MUSIC AT WESLEYAN

From Glee Club to Gamelan

Mark Slobin

MUSIC AT WESLEYAN

From Glee Club to Gamelan

WESLEYAN UNIVERSITY PRESS
MIDDLETOWN, CONNECTICUT

Published by Wesleyan University Press
Middletown, CT 06459
www.wesleyan.edu/wespress
© 2010 Mark Slobin

Library of Congress
Cataloging-in-Publication Data
Slobin, Mark.
Music at Wesleyan: from glee club to gamelan /
Mark Slobin.
      p. cm.
ISBN 978-0-8195-7078-9 (cloth: alk. paper)
1. Wesleyan University (Middletown,
Conn.)—Musical groups.   2. Musical groups—
Connecticut—Middletown—History.   I. Title.
ML33.M53W474 2010
780.71'17466—dc22
                              2010004452

Table of Contents

Welcome to one world.

This book, through its materials and energy, unleashes a remarkable panorama, just as music itself has done throughout Wesleyan's history.

Prior to the unfolding of Indian and Javanese and Japanese and Ghanaian and Afro-American musics at Wesleyan in the 1960s, the university had participated in a general exchange of students with other countries in Europe and Asia. Joe Beech, born in England and Wesleyan class of 1899, was admired for his work in China where he was president of Chengtu College (1905–1914) and chancellor of West China Union University (1914–1941) His work there led to student exchanges—indeed, my own college roommate, Dr. Donald G. Arnault, spent his junior year, 1938–1939, at West China Union University. The presence of Chinese students at Wesleyan is memorialized in the small Foss Hill Cemetery where two Chinese were buried after illness had struck them down—Fu-Sheng Chang in 1918 and Dieu Geing Wong in 1923. The one-worldness of Wesleyan music is perhaps symbolized by the fact that Joseph S. Daltry, founder of Wesleyan's music department, is laid to rest along with Fu-Sheng Chang and Dieu Geing Wong on Foss Hill.

Joe Daltry's importance to Wesleyan merits special attention. Born and reared in Australia, schooled in London and in Europe, he was Wesleyan's first full-time music professor, appointed in 1929. His job description required him to be chapel organist and choir master (at that time of paramount importance); to be director of the Glee Club; to introduce course work in classical music; and to teach classes in music theory—all of which he was exceedingly well-equipped to do. By the time I matriculated in 1936 he had firmly established a small, aggressive teaching/music-making department. His skill and commitment created a rock-solid foundation on which to build—without which Wesleyan's embrace of World Music could not have evolved.

What a pleasure that Mark Slobin had the instinct, energy, and skill to produce so lively a work as *Music at Wesleyan: From Glee Club to Gamelan*!

—*Richard K. Winslow '40*
John Spencer Camp Professor of Music, Emeritus

Author's Note

Wesleyan has always been a remarkably musical campus. By the late 1800s, it was called the "Singing College." The Glee Club toured regularly and extensively, earned positive reviews in the local presses of the hosting cities and towns, and won national awards. But the first faculty appointment in music did not arrive until the 1920s, and only two people taught music into the 1940s, rising to four by 1953.

The early 1960s saw a radical revolution in music that paralleled Wesleyan's opening from men's college to diverse university. A visionary program combining world music and experimental music vaulted Wesleyan to national and international prominence as a major center, unique among liberal arts colleges. Adding faculty to teach music from many cultures and a comprehensive graduate program, the department grew in numbers and in stature. Wesleyan's Music Department's undergrad alumni play in New York clubs, enter music graduate programs, compose film scores, teach music in many contexts, serve as state arts council chairs, foundation heads, or simply carry the joy and knowledge of music into their lives as a liberal arts legacy. Wesleyan's Music Department M.A. and Ph.D. graduates hold faculty positions across the U.S. and abroad, from Indonesia to India, from Africa to Australia, from Canada to Switzerland.

This book consists of two parts: pre- and post-1960s music at Wesleyan. I have been privileged to take part in nearly 20% of this grand musical pageant, and have greatly enjoyed assembling this brief account. It draws on images from Wesleyan University's Special Collections archives, for which I owe a huge round of thanks to its director, Suzy Taraba; to University photographer, John Wareham, for scans; and to music doctoral student, Jorge Arevalo Mateus, for researching *Argus* files. Bill Burkhart was enormously generous with photos; and Olivia Bartlett made the great suggestion of cleaning the North College plaques, to which John Meerts graciously acceded. I would like to thank Suzanna Tamminen and Leslie Starr of Wesleyan University Press for their instant embrace of celebrating the Wesleyan musical heritage, and foundational figure Richard Winslow for his informative and witty forays into department history.

All illustrations originated at Wesleyan, either from Special Collections or Public Information, so there are no specific caption credits. Most historical citations are from the student newspaper, the *Argus* (which tended not to feature bylines), unless otherwise indicated. I would like to thank the present and former faculty and students who offered the reminiscences quoted below. I would also like to thank Alec McLane and Dan Schnaidt for enabling the rich accompanying archive of online Wesleyan music over the decades. Copious thanks also go to Michael Roth for his generous support of this project.

To listen to performances of music at Wesleyan, you may access a selection of audio files at the companion digital archive for this book at http:wesscholar.wesleyan.edu/maw_audio/

PART ONE:

The Early Decades of the "Singing College"

Daniel G. Harriman of the class of 1864 wrote a song called "Greeting Glee" especially for a trip described as follows in the 1940 edition of the *Wesleyan Song Book*:

> *In the summer of 1862, the first regular Wesleyan Glee Club started afoot from Middletown for a trip to the White Mountains. The manager, Henry L. Dickinson '62, traveled a few hours ahead of the Club, making quick arrangements for lodging and concert hall at each evening's stopping place. The final concert was given on top of Mt. Washington.*

What a scene! A mere thirty years after the founding of Wesleyan, the elegantly-clad Glee Club is seen wandering on foot to the White Mountains, before the construction of Interstate 91 or the production of automobiles. Everywhere the singers stopped, people were glad to offer them food, lodging, and a concert hall to hear them sing. The foundations were being laid for the mythology of "The Singing College." Decade after decade, the singing young men ascended not just Mt. Washington, but the heights of the academic song world, winning the national intercollegiate championship back to

The Class of
1876, 1874.

1

back in 1926 and 1927. Also two years in a row, 1962 and 1963, Richard Winslow's men, combined with the Smith College women, went off to Mexico, courtesy of the State Department.

This heritage of song has largely faded from memory, but remains literally engraved at Wesleyan in the form of the plaques on the steps of North College. Everyone passes them by, and no one seems to notice them. A cleaning, specially done for this book, makes them more passably photogenic than before, though the names remain obscure to the Wesleyan community today. It is so striking that only songwriters are celebrated in so prominent a place on campus. No football heroes, debaters, presidents, or professors grace the steps.

The Glee Club was hardly the only outlet for undergraduate vocalizing. At all kinds of college events, the students raised their voices in song. Unfortunately, it is only the men we hear about; there is very little trace of women's musicality in the period from

North College plaques honor Wesleyan songwriters, 2008.

FOR THEIR CONTRIBUTIONS TO WESLEYAN MUSIC

WE HONOR

KARL POMEROY HARRINGTON '82
WESLEYAN SONG BOOK ASSOCIATE EDITOR

"SONG MEMORIES"

FREDERIC LAWRENCE KNOWLES '94

"O, IVIED WALLS..."
"SECRETS"

CARL FOWLER PRICE '02
WESLEYAN SONG BOOK EDITOR

"NOW THAT THE DAYS ARE MELLOW..."

CLIFFORD LeGRAND WAITE '06

"VICTORY" AND "BATTLE CRY"

THEIR SONGS WILL ALWAYS QUICKEN AND WARM
THE HEARTS OF WESLEYAN MEN, EVERYWHERE.

1872–1912 when Wesleyan was a coed college. The boys were always singing, it seems, since there were so many ritual events in the calendar for the couple or few hundred lucky members on campus each year. Below, a few choice examples of frolicking and solemnity evoke the importance of music at Wesleyan in the early decades, before the arrival of multicultural music and gender balance changed so much of the local resonance.

THE GLEE CLUB WORLD

What were the boys singing, when not atop Mt. Washington but back in the Chapel? The program for November 19, 1869, illustrates three kinds of pieces: college songs, classical music favorites—often from opera—and light fare. In a wry Wesleyan way, the composer of "Viva la Wesleyan" is given—misspelled—as "unbekannt," German for "anonymous," just as Pat Molloy's solo is ascribed to "umlaut," the German double-dot sign over o and u. "Johnny Schmauker," sometimes given as "Johnny Schmoker" in programs, looks like a German parody number of the type popular in that era. Whatever it symbolized, the song began its life at Wesleyan. According to an 1869 account in the *Western Collegian*, "'Johnny Schmoker' was first brought before the American public by the Glee Club of the Wesleyan University, Conn."

In today's a cappella age, opera seems a surprisingly large part of the repertoire of choice. In 1869, arias were popular music, widely distributed in the sheet music that most people kept in their homes as part of the common American habit of friends and family singing around the piano.

The reviews for the concert at the Tremont Temple in Boston speak eloquently to the fame Wesleyan's Glee Club had secured by 1884.

Tremont Temple.

COLLEGE BOYS

—AND—

COLLEGE SONGS.

—THE—

Wesleyan University Glee Club,

COMPOSED OF 18 VOICES,

—WILL GIVE A—

GRAND CONCERT

—OF—

COLLEGE SONGS, WARBLES AND CHORUSES,

—ON—

Monday Evening, June 2d, 1884.

PRESS NOTICES.

The singing was admirable; in fact, there is no discount on the excellence of the club. The programme was liberal to start with, but was stretched to considerable length by the replies to repeated encores. The performance reflected great credit on their trainer and conductor, John S. Camp.—*Springfield Republican*, Jan. 24, 1884.

The audience was enthusiastic, and applause was long and requent. A feature of the concert, and one that called forth several encores, was the warbling of Mr. G. D. Beatty, an imitation of the Swiss yodel.—*Worcester Times*, Feb. 2, '84.

If there are any better glee clubs in this country they have not come this way, and it is more than probable that the Wesleyan is positively the best. Their time is faultless, their enunciation excellent, their execution easy, and their harmony superb.—*Wilkes-Barre* (Pa.) *Record*, Dec. 29.

"Not even standing room" was the word at the door of the hall before the concert commenced. The singing of the club was excellent.—*Springfield Democrat*, Jan. 24, 1884.

The singing throughout was spirited, the voices well trained, and, taken as a whole, was one of the most satisfactory concerts ever given here—and that is saying a great deal.—*Hartford Post*.

The Wesleyan College Glee Club gave a very enjoyable concert in Music Hall last evening. The programme comprised glees, quartettes, solos, and instrumental music. The selections were frequently encored, and were rendered with a vim and a snap that made them peculiarly entertaining.—*Brooklyn Union and Argus*.

The concert by the Wesleyan College Glee Club at the Y. M. C. A. Hall last night gave entire satisfaction. The voices blended in an admirable manner, and the singing throughout showed evidence of careful training. The club, though comparatively unknown to Newarkers, is one of the very best that has as yet visited the city.—*Newark* (N.J.) *Advertiser*, Dec. 24.

Reserved Seats, 50 and 75 cts., according to location.

Tickets can be obtained at the Box Office, Tremont Temple, on and after Wednesday Morning, May 28.

Doors open at 7.15.	**Concert commences 7.45.**

RAND, AVERY & CO., PRINTERS, BOSTON.

W. U. G. C.

PROGRAMME.

Friday Evening, Nov. 19, '69.

PART I.

1. CHORUS, Oh hail us ye free—"Ernani." Verdi
2. University Song, - - - Harrington.
3. Solo and Chorus—Constantinople. Lloyd.
4. Chorus.—Night's shade no longer, "Moses in Egypt," - - - - - Rossini.
5. German Student Song.—Rodenstein, C. Herring.
6. Duett—On to the Field—Belisario. Donizetti.
7. Solo—Pat Malloy, - - - Umlaut.
8. Johnny Schmauker, - - - Harriman.

PART II.

1. Glee—Now Tramp o'er Moss and Fell, Bishop.
2. Solo and Chorus—Tapioca, - - Warden.
3. Duett—Larboard Watch, - T. Williams.
4. College Song—"Viva la Wesleyan." Unbekannt.
5. Quartette—Stars of the Summer Night. Müller.
6. College Chorus—Quodlibet. - Blish.
7. Medley. - - - - - Class of '67.
8. Glee—What phrase sad and soft. Bishop.

C. H. PELTON & SON, PRINT.

Glee Club
program, 1869.

Glee Club
program, 1884.

5

In Wilkes-Barre, Pennsylvania, the *Record* rates the group as "positively the best," an opinion seconded by the Newark *Advertiser*. The yodeling of Mr. G. D. Beatty, which he repeated numerous times on demand, was typical of the age. Traveling troupes of Swiss and Tyrolean Alpine singing families crisscrossed America as early as the 1850s.

The 1869 "Grand Union Concert" of the Yale and Wesleyan Glee Clubs, offers a rare chance to size up choruses side by side. This benefit concert featured solo and joint numbers, again with many German and classical items, as well as what we might call "novelty" pieces, such as "Solomon Levi," a very popular song we would certainly ban as anti-Semitic today. The bundling of a Spanish, Chinese, and probably Balkan ("Fatinitza") number speaks to other versions of ethnic and international stereotyping. What "The Pope" said about Catholicism is left to our imaginations. The second-half opener, "George Washington," rounds out the standard sampling of popular styles of the day, which always included the theme of patriotism.

The transportation is as eye-catching as the song list. One could simply take the train from Middletown to New Haven and back, and $1.00 would cover both ticket and transportation to and from the stations. Sometimes the old days were actually more convenient.

The Wesleyan students probably expected to come out on top in this Connecticut choral rivalry. Back in 1873, the *Argus* contentedly made this observation:

> *We clip the following from a Meriden paper: "We were somewhat disappointed at the singing of the Yale club, though in their college songs (their legitimate music) they did fairly. According to our humble judgement, the 'Wesleyans' of Middletown far surpass them.*

GRAND UNION CONCERT

BY THE

Yale and Wesleyan Glee Clubs

Wednesday Evening, April 23, 1884,

At Carll's Opera House, New Haven, Ct.

YALE GLEE CLUB.

Acting President, D. S. Knowlton.   *Business Manager, C. W. Cutler.*

First Tenor.	Second Tenor.
D. S. KNOWLTON.	D. A. JONES.
E. I. SANFORD, Jr.	F. D. BOWEN.
J. L. ADLER.	E. McCLELLAN.
J. BEADLE.	F. D. BRANDAGEE.

First Bass.	Second Bass.
W. H. JESSUP.	C. W. CUTLER.
A. P. WILDER.	W. P. BRANDAGEE.
F. STRONG.	G. S. WOODWARD.
H. HAND.	L. D. TOURTELLOT.

WESLEYAN GLEE CLUB.

President, J. S. Camp.   *Secretary, A. L. Green.*

First Tenor.	Second Tenor.
F. C. HOYT.	P. F. ELA.
F. T. TATEUM.	G. D. BEATTYS.
F. W. SMITH.	A. E. LOOMIS.
F. W. BOUTON.	J. C. CONVERSE.
S. N. TAYLOR.	

First Bass.	Second Bass.
W. A. TATEUM.	G. A. CARNAHAN.
J. F. FELLOWS.	L. J. MAGEE.
J. A. SAXE.	J. C. CLARK.
	W. E. WOODRUFF.

☞ **THE ENTIRE PROCEEDS OF THIS CONCERT TO BE DEVOTED TO A CHARITABLE OBJECT.** ☜

✶PROGRAMME✶

PART FIRST.

1. "LAURIGER." — BOTH CLUBS.
2. WEIMAR FOLK SONG, - - - Liszt
3. SWEET VIOLETS, — Solo, Mr. W. TATEUM. Warble, Mr. BEATTYS.
4. MARCH, - - - Becker — YALE.
5. { I WISH I WERE A— / FRA DIAVOLO.
6. MAID OF ATHENS. — Tenor-Solo, Mr. F. TATEUM.
7. { DIE LORELEI, / DAYLIGHT, — With warble by Mr. ADLER. YALE.
8. SOLDIER'S FAREWELL.

PART SECOND.

1. GEORGE WASHINGTON. — YALE.
2. LOOK! LOOK! — With warble by Mr. BEATTYS.
3. { SOLOMON LEVI. / GUITAR SONG. — With Baritone Solo and Warble.
4. AVE MARIA, - - - - Abt — Solo by Mr. KNOWLTON. YALE.
5. LAUGH, BOYS, LAUGH.
6. { SPANISH STUDENT. / CHINESE SONG.
7. FATINITZA. — Whistle by Mr. JONES. YALE.
8. THE POPE. — BOTH CLUBS.

Tickets, - - 50 Cents	A Special Train will leave Middletown at 6.30 P. M. Return at close of Concert.
Reserved Seats, - $1.00	Tickets for the trip and Concert, $1.00
For sale at LOOMIS' TEMPLE OF MUSIC, New Haven, Ct.	Reserved Seats, - 50 cents extra.
Friday, April 18, 1884.	For sale at HAZEN'S BOOK STORE, Middletown, Ct.
	Thursday, April 17, 1884.

Yale and Wesleyan Glee Clubs Joint Concert program, 1869.

We have all kinds of sources that support this boosterism. Take the account of the 1899 Glee and Mandolin Club trips, which took twenty-five students south to New Jersey, Pennsylvania, West Virginia, and Washington D.C.: "The trip covered in all about nineteen hundred miles, and the clubs traveled the entire route in a private [train] car. … The first concert was given in the YMCA Hall, Philadelphia, before an audience of over thirteen hundred." Arriving at the nation's capital, the students received the ultimate welcome from William McKinley: "The President received the clubs informally in the cabinet room for a few moments, shaking hands with each man." They then gave a concert at the Metropolitan church, of which McKinley was a member. Various wives of senators, congressmen, and judges organized the event. In that era, it was women who made sure concert life was a strong part of local entertainment, even at the highest levels of government.

The 1901 Christmas trip yielded the same results. At a concert in Camden, New Jersey, "Almost every number was enthusiastically encored, and just before the last, the clubs were given a fine ovation. The whole audience of nearly two thousand rose to their feet and cheered and waved a salute for several minutes." The President was just as welcoming, but there was a hitch: "President McKinley received the clubs in the cabinet room of the White House. At that time he expressed regret that it had been necessary to cancel [his] invitation for a concert on Monday … and urged the clubs to stay another day [which they couldn't do due to a concert in Camden]. He promised, however, to hear the clubs sing next June, when he proposes to visit Wesleyan."

Perhaps McKinley would have made good on that promise, but he was destined not to hear the clubs again, as he met an assassin's bullet a short time later, in September of that year.

Glee Club
Octet on Tour
at Chautauqua,
1888.

Given the great prestige of glee clubs, it is not surprising that many students tried to form one, and that not all of them had an easy time finding their niche, though one group of 1873 managed a breakthrough:

We well remember under what inauspicious circumstances the Arion Glee Club was organized. Various were the predictions as to their fate. Some few prophetic ones foretold for them a most "inglorious fizzle." Others, feeling that the college greatly needed a glee club, gave them their best wishes, but could offer few words of encouragement … they persevered with commendable zeal, till success crowned their efforts. Everywhere they sang, they found an appreciative audience. For two years on many public occasions connected with the college, they have furnished excellent music, free, gratis. Thus many a dime has lingered yet a little longer in our pockets ere it went the way of all the rest.

Such was the power of glee clubs that part of the profits from their tours went to support athletic programs, an unthinkable system given today's primacy of athletics on American college campuses. An 1889 program includes a "Base Ball Bulletin" that demonstrates this linkage.

Durability marks the history of glee clubs. In 1911, we see that "a picked Quartette from 'The Singing College of New England' is offering pretty much the same fare as their predecessors decades earlier: classical music, German numbers, exotic novelty pieces, and comic items to present "an ideal entertainment with an abundance of humor." Some of that fun must have come in "De Coppah Moon," clearly a minstrel-show item that is either written by a different poet named Shelley or is a travesty of the great Romantic poet's work, a tradition dating back to the Shakespeare spoofs of the mid-nineteenth century.

Glee Club
Quartette
Program, 1911.

The Jibers,
1911–12 season,
undated.

We see strong continuity in even the physical presence of the Wesleyan a cappella groups of yore. The Jibers not only lasted for decades, but kept the same outfits and hairstyles over the forty-five years from the time the 1911–12 photo was taken to the 1956–57 photo shoot.

THE JIBERS 1956–57
Voss,T.'57; Hall,J.'58; Van Norman,D.'57; Allen,J.'57.

The Jibers,
1956–57 season,
undated.

THE '88 GLEE CLUB

THEODORE RICHARDS, *President*

H. P. GRIFFIN, *Business Manager*

RICHMOND P. PAINE, *Musical Director*

First Tenor

M. W. GILL, '89
E. S. FERNALD, '90
E. A. NOBLE, '90
F. A. BAGNALL, '90

Second Tenor

H. P. GRIFFIN, '88
T. A. HUMASON, '88
H. K. MUNROE, '88
J. M. HARRIS, '90

First Bass

THEO. RICHARDS, '88
S. V. COFFIN, '89
W. A. MONTGOMERY, '90
R. B. HIBBARD, '91

Second Bass

G. D. HAMLEN, '88
F. M. DAVENPORT, '89
H. L. CAMPBELL, '90
L. E. LA FETRA, '91

DURING the college year 1887-88 this club gave twenty-two concerts, as follows:

NEW LONDON, CONNECTICUT	WILKES-BARRE, PENNSYLVANIA
TERRYVILLE, CONNECTICUT	BERWICK, PENNSYLVANIA
WELLESLEY, MASSACHUSETTS	DANVILLE, PENNSYLVANIA
AUBURNDALE, MASSACHUSETTS	COLUMBIA, PENNSYLVANIA
NEW BRITAIN, CONNECTICUT	OLD POINT COMFORT, VIRGINIA
MIDDLETOWN, CONNECTICUT	WASHINGTON, DISTRICT COLUMBIA
HARTFORD, CONNECTICUT	CHAMBERSBURG, PENNSYLVANIA
(with Amherst Club)	BROOKLYN, NEW YORK
ELIZABETH, NEW JERSEY	WINDSOR, CONNECTICUT
MONTCLAIR, NEW JERSEY	NEW YORK, NEW YORK
SCRANTON, PENNSYLVANIA	BRIDGEPORT, CONNECTICUT
MIDDLETOWN, CONNECTICUT	

Besides the above, the Octette from the Club gave concerts in Waterbury, Connecticut, and Wilbraham, Massachusetts, and in the summer of 1888 made a trip of 2,000 miles, singing before 15,000 people in the following places:

RED BANK, NEW JERSEY	FORT EDWARD, NEW YORK
ATLANTIC HIGHLANDS, NEW JERSEY	COTTAGE CITY, MASSACHUSETTS
CHAUTAUQUA, NEW YORK	VINEYARD HAVEN, MASSACHUSETTS
ROUND LAKE, NEW YORK	EDGARTOWN, MASSACHUSETTS
NANTUCKET, MASSACHUSETTS	

The repertoire of the Club included over sixty selections and it was classed as the best college glee club of its time. In connection with the seventy-fifth anniversary celebration of Wesleyan's founding, the '88 Club is holding its first re-union; and, through the courtesy of the undergraduate musical organizations, it is accorded a place upon the concert program. The members beg the indulgence of their friends while they " have a try " at some of the old songs, after a single rehearsal together.

Fortieth Reunion of the 1888 Glee Club program, 1926.

The fellowship of song created a lifelong tie for the boys who turned into men. Looking at the 1888 glee club's fortieth reunion photo, we see a group of men who look comfortable and at ease. They keep the formal attire and—for those that aren't balding—hairstyle of their youth as they advance into what was then nearly old age—their early sixties. The program for the 1926 event offers details of the group's accomplishments.

Glee Club,
1889.

Fortieth
Reunion of the
1888 Glee Club
group photo,
1926.

15

The Glee Club won the national championship in 1926, an event that tells us just how important such organizations were on campus nationwide.

What did the group sing as it battled its way to victory? The program is heavy on classical music, with a hymn, and leavened only by "Gipsy John," perhaps a version of an old British ballad about the lady who leaves her lord for a "Gipsy." The listing of "orchestra" shows the continuity of instrumentalists alongside vocalists. This might be the "Trio" of piano, violin, and flute, as opposed to "The Serenaders," who offer music for "dancing until 1 A.M.," played by a jazz-age combo of saxophones, trumpet, sousaphone, drums, and banjo.

The Glee Club's stability and primacy clearly has to do with its important function as an outreach and recruitment tool for the College, as already noted in 1899, the year of the first White House reception:

Intercollegiate Glee Club championship plaque, 1926.

The Glee Club, although not receiving so great public recognition as some of the other branches of student activity, has it in its power to do fully as much good for the college. It is no small advantage to have a good [g]lee [c]lub make an occasional incursion into regions where we are little known. Singing Wesleyan songs is certainly a far more effective manner of calling attention to the college than are circulars and advertisements, and often men are influenced by this means who could be reached in no other way.

PROGRAM

———

1. (a) Campus Song .... Magee '85
   (b) Land-Sighting .... Grieg
   GLEE CLUB

2. (a) Second Nocturne .... Behr
   (b) Pastorale .... Hillman
   TRIO

3. (a) "Thou art repose" .... Schubert
   (b) Shadow March .... Protheroe
   (c) From the Land of Sky-blue Water .... Cadman
   GLEE CLUB

4. (a) Prelude Op. 3, No. 2 .... Rachmaninoff
   (b) Valse Brilliante, No. 2 .... Godard
   M. D. CASNER

5. (a) Where'er You Walk .... Handel
   (b) Amici
   GLEE CLUB

Intermission

6. (a) Twilight Song .... Waite '06
   (b) It is the Lord's own day .... Kreutzer
   (c) The Broken Melody .... Sibelius
   GLEE CLUB

7. The Jibers
   MALE QUARTET

8. (a) The Long Day Closes .... Sullivan
   (b) Gipsy John .... Clay
   GLEE CLUB

9. The Serenaders
   ORCHESTRA

10. Alma Mater .... Davis '93
    GLEE CLUB

Dancing until 1 A. M.   Music by the Serenaders.

Wesleyan University Musical Clubs — 1927–28

———

G. L. Langreth '28, *Manager*   H. B. Matthews '28, *Leader*
D. H. Savage '29, *Assistant Manager*   E. F. Laubin, *Coach*

GLEE CLUB

FIRST BASS	FIRST TENOR
L. P. Gallivan '28	M. D. Casner '30
J. A. Kouwenhoven '31	V. B. Harrison '28
F. J. Lipsky '31	S. A. Larrabee '28
C. B. Mitchell '28	T. W. Millspaugh '30
E. F. Singer '30	L. J. Patricelli '29
W. M. F. Sleichter '30	C. W. Phy '30
R. E. Will '29	L. R. Theismeyer '28
	L. R. Thompson '28
	C. P. Torrance '31

SECOND BASS	SECOND TENOR
W. T. Carlson '28	D. M. Chapman '28
T. M. Church '31	R. A. Friend '30
J. D. Anthony '28	L. R. Holmes '30
E. L. Gaylor, Jr. '28	H. C. Knight '29
T. A. Hart '30	F. J. Landolt '30
H. J. Moss '31	C. Staples '29
C. J. Nordstrom '28	F. B. Stover '31
E. Reisner '31	J. R. Swain '29
H. H. Schwerdtle '28	A. F. Anderson '31
W. W. Torrey '29	

L. P. Gallivan '28, Soloist

SERENADERS

J. G. Campbell '30, Manager, Drums	T. J. Moss '30, Saxophone
R. A. Friend '30, Leader, Saxophone	R. N. Ryley '30, Trumpet
D. K. Hall '31, Sousaphone	R. F. Smith '30, Banjo
J. M. Millerick '28, Piano	S. Susselman '30, Saxophone

TRIO

M. D. Casner '30, Piano   L. J. Patricelli '29, Violin
R. N. Ryley '30, Flute

JIBERS

First Bass — W. M. F. Sleichter '30   First Tenor — V. B. Harrison '28
Second Bass — H. B. Matthews '28   Second Tenor — M. D. Casner '30

PIANO SOLOIST
M. D. Casner, '30

Glee Club program, 1927.

INSTRUMENTAL MUSIC

The "singing college" was also the strumming, bowing, and blowing college. Among the earliest data we have of music at Wesleyan is the 1838 music book of the Speirachordeon band.

Marches were common at social events and dances, not just athletic contests in those days. While 1838 is a shade early for photographs, by 1870 we have a fine picture of the band, sporting a varied assortment of instruments. With their mixture of strings, woodwinds, and brass, they could have played any music of the day, from dance tunes and sentimental songs to athletic and patriotic strains.

The public band lasted many decades, moving onto Andrus Field for football games. The tradition has receded in recent times, but is sometimes revived as the "pep band."

Speirachordeon Band's "Wesleyan March," 1838.

As on many campuses of the time, the Banjo Club stayed active for many years. An 1890 photo captures a nattily dressed group of four banjo players, three guitarists, and a mandolin player, in an era when the banjo was shifting from its rowdy minstrel-show roots to parlor gentility featuring a more classical repertoire.

The public band
on Andrus Field,
undated.

The Banjo Club,
1890.

Other photos indicate that students were fond of their instruments, even outside of band practice. The Class of 1876 chose to be pictured with their instruments—along with a hunting rifle and various ceremonial objects—in an 1874 photo.

Also in the picture are the first four women to be enrolled at Wesleyan, a practice that continued through the Class of 1912. Unfortunately, we have really no indication of women's musical role over those forty years. Doubtless they accompanied the male singers, as piano playing became an unavoidable "accomplishment" for all girls in the nineteenth century. They also formed their own drama groups that probably featured songs, as in this undated performance photo for the Gilbert and Sullivan operetta, *The Pirates of Penzance*.

Women and
men perform
together in
*The Pirates of
Penzance*. The
seated figure is
Frank Kierman,
'35, costumed
as the Major
General,
undated.

Peter Frenzel meets a new South College bell, 2005.

Perhaps the most stable instrumental music has been the sound of the South College bells. Professor Peter Frenzel has been their most devoted twenty-first century champion, spearheading their renovation and providing this capsule history:

> *The first eleven bells in the South College tower were given by the class of 1863 and dedicated in 1919. In 1966 an anonymous gift provided funds for five additional bells. Later it transpired that the donor was Victor L. Butterfield, then in the last year of his presidency of Wesleyan. With the Butterfield bells a new keyboard system was also installed in the standardized form of present-day chimes and carillons.*

The bells were rung sporadically at noon and before and after commencement until 2000, when several enthusiastic students founded the ringers' guild, Bell and Scroll. The ringing schedule was regularized so that the bells were rung every weekday noon hour during the academic year. In 2002 one of the guild members, Mariah Klaneski '04 produced a CD of the South College bells entitled "Thirteen O'Clock."

In the same year a fund drive was begun to raise $200,000 to buy and install an additional eight bells. The money was raised, the bells were mounted, and the dedication was held in November of 2005. The South College Chime had been transformed to a carillon (23 or more bells).

Bell & Scroll presently (2008) consists of eight ringers with several more apprentices. The guild members play at the noon-hour, and for special events such as weddings or memorial services, and throughout the day during Reunion and Commencement weekend.

Installing the
new bells,
2005.

THE CEREMONIAL MUSIC WORLD

Old Wesleyan, with its small, homogeneous student body, favored a variety of ceremonial moments that have long gone out of fashion. Class Day, held around the time of commencement, was one of those, and both the ritual and musical moments it sparked seem far from today's idea of campus life, as for example in this description from 1868:

> About 2:30 P.M. the class formed a circle under the mulberry tree, near Rich Hall, where they were surrounded by the rest of the college and a large number of friends. First came a song entitled "Retrospect," beginning:
>
> > O mores! Tempora! now do, Fol de rol, etc.
> > Just smile again before we go, Fol de rol, etc.
> > and sung to the exhilarating air "I-Eel."
>
> … Next came the dubbing of the Grand Panjandrum of the Knights of the Silver Cup. Nast, as master of ceremonies, placed upon Dusinberre, the Grand Panjandrum, the emblems of the order, and gave him an accolade with an elegant wooden sword. After singing a song commencing
>
> > The days of college life we sing. Aha!
> > Let memory 'round our history cling. For Sixty-Eight, Hurrah!
> > Till all is up with everything. Aha! Aha! Aha!
>
> … After a brief intermission spent in brushing black clothes and polishing silk hats, the class assembled for the usual FAREWELL EXERCISES.
>
> … The class of '68 smoked the pipe of peace beneath a beautiful maple in front of the college. It was one of those never-to-be-forgotten scenes which come

*only now and then in a lifetime .... [A]fter enjoying the "Pipe Song," came the
address to the college ... a dignified, chaste, and elegant production, gracefully
delivered .... The singing of a humorous medley, entitled "Sammi Brent,"
completed the exercise on the campus.*

The Peace Pipe ritual did not always go off perfectly. Just one year later, the students
couldn't get the pipe lit. The ready access to someone's well-used fine meerschaum pipe
indicates just how entrenched tobacco was in college life:

*At 3:30 P.M. the boys formed their circle under the shade of the maple in front of
the college and sang their first song. After this followed the "Smoking of the Pipe
of Peace." But although George E. had charge of the fine Turkish bowl it would
not smoke; so they got a redolent and tried old meerschaum and passed it round.*

*The singing in the evening was admirable. Not so much volume as '68 but much
sweeter .... Porter's sweet voice struck out these beautiful words, to that beautiful
melody, "The Maltese Boatman's Song."*

*Sadly we list for the midnight chime
Tolling, farewell, Sixty-Nine*

Tobacco was the headliner at the "Smoker," a common music-ceremonial event not tied
to a specific date on the college calendar, as in this 1899 account:

*Cigars, cigarettes and tobacco were in abundance, sandwiches and lemonade
were served, and the evening was given up to social chat and genial fellowship.
Mr. Tasker rendered two violin solos, with piano accompaniment by Mr. Smith,
and a farce was given by Messrs. Hurlbut and C. H. Davis. College singing was
a prominent feature of the evening. Everybody present voiced the sentiment that
the occasion was the most delightful college event of the year.*

On display here is the common taste that infused all events: a combination of the more classical violin and piano pieces, the comedic, the farce, and the ever-present college songs.

College songs were a national mania, and an enormous amount of energy went into their composition and collection, as described in this article from 1901:

The Song Book Committee met on Saturday morning to organize for regular work. It is the purpose of the board to publish a book of 100 pages. Enough material for about 50 pages is now on hand. To complete the book a number of songs, which are not distinctively Wesleyan songs but are more or less common to all colleges, will be used. A considerable number of new songs, however, are yet to be written.

Two Wesleyan songbook covers, from 1914 and 1940, are similarly simple in design, though the first seems more local, giving W. B. Davis as composer, while the later edition, put out by an "intercollegiate" publisher, seems more generalized. The 1914 version of Davis's song in honor of John Wesley—but celebrating "Mother Wesleyan"—features a title in Latin, adding a mock-classic tinge.

Wesleyan songbook covers, 1914 and 1940.

"Carmen Iohannis Weslii," or "John Wesley's Song," by W. B. Davis, '94, from *Wesleyan Songs*, 1914.

Classical music was not completely neglected on campus; it just mixed with popular, even in the official organ recitals designed to draw a general audience to the Chapel. Some reviews stress the importance of the more serious selections, as this one from 1899:

> *The first of the series of three organ recitals highly pleased the audience of two hundred people who assembled in Memorial Chapel. Mr. C. R. Smith's performances upon the organ never fail to delight the lovers of music. His renderings are marked by an accuracy and fineness of touch and never lack character. There was great variety in his selections. Schubert's "Serenade" found particular favor with those fond of minor music while Mendelssohn's "War March of the Priests" was the favorite of others.*

Despite the attempt to make the organ recital a base for classical music, this style was not necessarily a big draw on its own, as this lament from 1873 tells us:

> *Theodore Thomas's orchestra gave one of their unrivaled concerts at Hartford ... about seventy-five excursionists from the city attended, and returned after the entertainment on a special train. We were very sorry to see so small a delegation from the college. The crowd will go to a "Combination Troupe" or a "negro Minstrel Troupe" five nights in a week, but can't see any enjoyment in a musical entertainment of real merit. The great want is a cultivated taste, instead of one vitiated by such "shows" as frequent our public halls.*

Theodore Thomas (1835–1905), a German immigrant, was a mighty force in the development of the American symphony orchestra, and would have been a celebrated figure at the time.

The taste for light entertainment flowed naturally from the more frivolous side of college life, occasionally critiqued in the pages of the *Argus* as early as 1869:

> *The student of the period is a gay and festive individual .... He has a penchant for billiards and poker, and regard with curious disdain the man who refuses to drink. He swears like a trooper; is an habitue of traveling minstrel shows, and an ardent admirer of tatterdemalion concert troupes ... he has oyster suppers, his wines, his horses, in short, is a man of the world."*

Ceremonial musical occasions tried to anchor the free-floating student social atmosphere. But even the most high-minded events could be undercut by high jinks. The most important regularly scheduled musical ritual was Chapel, which was required. Lest we assume that services were always sober and serious, descriptions like this one of 1873 reveal what really went on:

A VINDICATION OF THE COLLEGE CHOIR

> *There are men in our midst, we are sorry to say, of such eccentricity as to believe that members of a choir are equally responsible with the congregation for good order and proper conduct during the service. Who ever heard of such an idea? Did you ever know of a choir that did not indulge freely in laughter and conversation, and all manner of merriment, throughout the sermon, and especially during prayer? And can you rightly expect more from ours?*

Sacred and secular ceremonial music alternated and combined freely on campus year-round. One patriotic ritual that has been lost today, but very important in Wesleyan's past, was George Washington's birthday, February 22. An 1869 account tells us that "'Washington's Birthday,' 'Gathering of the Free,' 'American Ensign,' and 'Star Spangled Banner' ... were rendered with energy and taste and apparently much to the satisfaction of the audience." We take "The Star Spangled Banner" for granted as core musical

Americana, but at that time, the song was still thirty years from its first official use, by the U.S. Navy in 1800, and 62 years would elapse until it became the national anthem in 1931. Yet it was widely sung, played, and even danced to in the period.

To round out this brief glimpse of early Wesleyan music, here is a philosophical account of campus life from 1869. The comment about the American Indian origins of music seems almost to presage the arrival of Native American music on campus nearly eight decades later:

It is said that music was invented by an Indian, who got lost from his tribe and wanted something to amuse himself with … yes, music is a mighty nice thing, especially in college … how cheering for the lonely freshman, digging for classic treasures by the midnight oil, to be serenaded by an admiring multitude, whose notes betray the enthusiasm of hero-worshippers …

No music is more pleasing and popular, none more profitable to the singers and attractive to the hearers, than college music. But it is as apparent as [it is] lamentable that singing zeal in our University is on the decline … so to speak, we have hung our harps upon the willows; but as baseball and boating are out of season at present, we hope that neglected Euterpe will again receive the attention which she merits. From the ashes of our dead glee clubs and musical associations we fondly expect to see new ones arise as attractive and popular as those of other days …. Serenades are far less common here than in most college neighborhoods, not because we have less talent or less gallantry, but for the want of precedent.

But we will pause. A word to the wise is sufficient. Music, as well as murder, will out, and let it come, I repeat it, let it come.

(We have failed to observe any special indications of that decline of "singing zeal" among us remarked by the writer of the above article. —Ed.)

The editor's optimism was fully borne out by the many decades of energetic song and ceremony that followed this column. In some ways, it seems that not much changed. In 1944, the *Argus* indicates that campus musical taste still leaned towards popular song, and that smoking was quite commonplace:

> *The average Wesleyan man has a leaning toward lively brunettes, listens to Bob Hope with great faith, smokes Chesterfield cigarettes, abominates John L. Lewis, and has great confidence in President Franklin Delano Roosevelt .... Frank Sinatra topped Adolph Hitler by three votes to become the second greatest "poisonality" of the year [after the President].*

All this is very masculine in orientation. As noted above, we know next to nothing about the role of women in campus music, even during the early decades of coeducation. We read about women as prom dates. To take one example, the wartime year of 1944 finds the fraternities scrambling to get a prom going, due to the lack of manpower with so many boys out fighting, but nevertheless putting together the required dating list:

> *Fraternity Houses will be allowed to stage dances on Friday evening, January 21, providing that the dance is over at 12:00 midnight and the girls are out of the House before 1 A.M. The names of the chaperones for such an affair have to be in the Dean's office one week before the dance.*

> *It had first been proposed to have a big name orchestra but this idea was voted down on the grounds that there were not enough students on campus to support such an undertaking successfully.*

> *Ninety-nine girls will be the dates of Wesleyan students for the Winter Prom this weekend, according to the names indicated on the traditional dance lists ....*

Wesleyan men have indicated their preference for girls from Smith College and from Middletown, according to the dance list, since there will be more girls present from these two places than from other colleges or cities.

Smith College was more than just a source of dates for Wesleyan. Under the leadership of Richard Winslow, '40, who was hired into the Music Department in 1949, the Wesleyan Glee Club reached a new golden age, partly through his highly successful partnership with Ivy Dee Hiatt, the Smith choir leader. The two groups toured together, and in 1962 and 1963 they gladly accepted an invitation from the State Department to tour Mexico.

The Choral Blue Yonder: Wesleyan-Smith Glee Club tour to Mexico, 1962.

Richard Winslow leading the mixed Wesleyan-Smith Glee clubs, 1960.

Informal women's singing group, undated.

Winslow's success was both organizational and aesthetic as he energized the campus's vocal traditions. His approach, based on "the elemental notion that the sound ought to be propelled *not* by the throat/mouth area but by the body of the singer," was emphatically nontraditional. He also expanded the repertoire, including his own compositions, as well as his arrangements of pieces by American music's pioneer radical, Charles Ives.

Eventually, the need to join choral forces with Smith College evaporated as Wesleyan admitted women in 1970. The new version of choral singing brought gender balance to music at Wesleyan, in both formal and informal settings.

Richard Donohue and the Concert Choir, 1970s.

The arrival of female musicians coincided with Winslow's interest in a more expansive musical sensibility for Wesleyan, and the numeric growth of the music department. In 1944, the time of the fraternity dances just described, the Music Department had two faculty members: Joseph Daltry, the first appointment in music, hired in 1929, and Fritz Sternfeld. They offered a total of seven courses. By 1953, the department roster had swelled to four, including Winslow and the much-beloved teacher Ray Rendall, who began in 1952.

Ray Rendall teaching a piano student, 1960s(?).

Under Winslow's leadership and with the collaboration of David McAllester, an anthropologist-ethnomusicologist hired in 1947, the department embarked on a visionary quest to create an entirely new formation unparalleled at any liberal arts college even today. Eventually called the "World Music Program," this new, dramatic phase of music at Wesleyan began around 1960. Its story follows.

PART TWO:

The World Music Era: 1960 and Beyond

Something very surprising happened in the world of music at Wesleyan, beginning in the late 1940s, when David McAllester and Richard Winslow were hired (1947 and 1949 respectively). McAllester was the leading authority on the music of the Navajo people, and one of the four founders of the Society for Ethnomusicology. He taught liberal arts right across the board, in the Wesleyan way, including great books, psychology, and anthropology, starting both of the last two departments. Winslow was a radical New Englander and a Wesleyan grad who had been to Juilliard and spent time in Panama during World War II. Together, McAllester and Winslow changed not just local but national and international music history by envisioning a dramatic new direction for the school's tiny music department.

As Winslow tells it, "all through the 1950s, David was brainwashing me" to expand towards world music. Meanwhile, he himself was being influenced by the new currents sweeping American music composition, notably in the work of John Cage, who came to Wesleyan and performed a highly dramatic concert, a story beautifully

Taiko drumming at commencement, 2008.

35

told by Winslow:

John Cage first visited Wesleyan in 1955, with David Tudor, to play a concert of his two-piano music written for the then-notorious "prepared" piano—an instrument whose tone had been altered by plugging the strings with such objects as nuts, bolts, rubber erasers, wood sticks, etc., carefully chosen and placed. In those days students had to get ten chapel or assembly credits per semester and any event late in a semester would be heavily attended. The Public Relations Office ... publicized the concert as featuring SKREWBALL PIANISTS. The chapel was mobbed.

Cage, responding to the teeming hall like fire horse to fire, commenced proceedings with a devastating surprise: he delivered a ten-minute lecture, in voice so quiet that even in the front row one had to strain to hear, about the probable impact on music of the then-new electromagnetic tape. The audience, expecting Spike Jones [a music satirist] but hearing a science lecture, was badly thrown off balance.

When the music started with its galaxies of strange, even shocking sounds, the hall turned into a contained madhouse. Some stuffed handkerchiefs into their mouths to prevent vocal disgrace, others turned red in the face with anger at the laughers, all were galvanized either by fascination or outrage.

When at intermission Mr. Cage calmly said "we will now re-prepare the pianos for the second half and any who wish may come up to watch us," the hall exploded. Students struggled to get to the stage, some even running across the tops of pews and standing on top of the grand pianos to view the procedures. During the second half, a few left in anger, only to return out of determination not to be driven away and by the end of the concert, there was a general feeling of disorientation combined with an exhilaration that must also have been present after the first performance of Stravinsky's Rite of Spring in 1913 in Paris, when there were riots and the police had to intervene.

In 1960, Cage became one of the first Fellows at Wesleyan's Center for Advanced Studies (now Center for the Humanities) and spent the academic year there. He returned for the second semester of 1969. In 1961, Wesleyan University Press published Cage's *Silence,* surely the most important book by a twentieth-century American composer. In 1988, the Music Department threw a grand festival for Cage on the occasion of his seventy-fifth birthday, attracting stellar musicians and fellow composers in one of the most memorable music events ever held on campus. Wesleyan students have been

John Cage
and Richard
Winslow with
the Wesleyan
Orchestra,
1974.

presenting his music for a very long time, as this anecdote from faculty composer Alvin Lucier relates:

Sometime in the late Eighties I took a group of Wesleyan students and alumni down to Walter Damrosch Park at Lincoln Center to perform John Cage's Cartridge Music. In that piece pipe cleaners, toothpicks, bobby pins and other such objects are inserted into phonograph cartridges and amplified enormously. After we had gotten into the performance for a few minutes, about half the audience got up and left. Cage said his music was like insect spray on an audience. A few flits and everyone scatters. It's a terrific piece.

John Cage and Neely Bruce at the Cage Festival, 1988.

WORLD MUSIC TAKES ROOT
AND FLOURISHES

Cage's appearance was not the only new departure for the emerging campus music scene. In the early 1960s, the legendary Indian musician, Ravi Shankar, stopped at Wesleyan on one of his earliest tours to the United States. His visit marked an important milestone on the road to Wesleyan's future World Music Program.

Ravi Shankar at the Memorial Chapel, 1961(?).

Winslow and McAllester got the go-ahead to hire a full-time ethnomusicologist, and they found Robert E. Brown, who had just graduated from the very first academic world music program, which was offered at UCLA. The campus quickly noticed a new spirit, as reported by an alumni magazine reporter in 1964:

> A bearded, quiet young man named Robert E. Brown introduced the South Indian or Carnatic music at Wesleyan in 1961. In a manner so gentle that he might have been expected to cause few ripples on the campus, he has generated so much activity and interest in a completely strange subject that it is not unusual to hear the remark: "Wait till you see what Brown's got going now."

Here is a snapshot of the music scene of the early 1960s. Much music making was done in informal spaces (like kitchens) in the years before the Center

"Demonic virtuosity that virtually toppled the senses." —N. Y. HERALD TRIBUNE

"Musical excitement...superb performance... audience burst into cheers by the end of the second selection." —N. Y. TIMES

RAVI SHANKAR

INDIA'S GREAT SITARIST AND COMPOSER

KANAI DUTTA, with N. C. MULLICK,
tabla   tamboura

FIRST COAST-TO-COAST
AMERICAN TOUR
presented by
THE ASIA SOCIETY
PERFORMING ARTS PROGRAM

Presented by WESLEYAN UNIVERSITY
MEMORIAL CHAPEL
Saturday, October 14 at 8:00 P.M.
ADMISSION BY CONCERT SERIES TICKET ONLY

for the Arts was built. Dick Winslow, driving spirit of the department, has his pipe; and Jon Higgins, an undergrad who much later returned to become Director of the Center for the Arts and Dean of Division I, sports the usual cigarette of the day. Bob Brown, who engineered the great growth of the department in the 1960s ran a series of "curry concerts" in his house, a Wesleyan-owned barn, where he cooked food alongside resident faculty from India.

Bob Brown's World Music Kitchen, early 1960s.

Sometime during this era, a book appeared in India lamenting the decline of their classical music and praising a college in America where the professor and musicians not only teach music, but live and cook with students. The authors cite Wesleyan as a utopian model India should learn from. Winslow's report to the Trustees of 1966 summarizes what went on in the early 1960s frankly and colorfully:

When Brown arrived in autumn 1961, things began to happen fast. He and McAllester jointly offered a survey of world music. Brown established a study group in Indian music, made the case that we couldn't teach the stuff without instruments, and we bought some. Interest grew. Soon we were faced with the situation that you could take students only so far without the presence of native teachers, and we began acquiring them .... We sent two brilliant boys to India on Fulbrights .... One of our students wrote a cross-cultural opera which

40

received a major performance at the Loeb Theatre at Harvard with Wesleyan students playing and singing, traveling virtuosi such as Ali Akbar Kahn [sic] began dropping in to see what was going on, etc., etc. Then came the move to establish a doctoral program, it made sense, and is now underway. To provide proper support for a doctoral program we needed to add a western musicologist, and I think we got a lulu in young Jon Barlow.

Jon Barlow meets Beethoven. This bust stayed in the department lobby for decades, 1970s.

Jon Barlow: Early Music and the Liberal Arts, undated.

41

We needed more breadth in world offerings, so we now have three Indian artists (singer, drummer, vina player, all absolutely of the first rank), a fine Japanese koto player, a Japanese musicologist who also did three years research in Persia, a professor in Sanskrit and—coming next year—an expert in linguistics.

I think we are pioneering a fantastically fruitful area. I predict that within ten years our example will have been widely emulated and within twenty-five years it will have become a norm. It is in our view, not only eminently logical but almost frustratingly necessary. We are grateful, we are <u>very</u> grateful, that Wesleyan University, its administration, trustees, and indeed its faculty generally, had the flexibility, good humor, good sense, faith, to allow the beginning to be made. There have been some trying times, there has been some exotic behavior, there have been galloping expenses.

All this ought to be going on in the presence of experimental music: experimental, avant-garde music is an international language, it is the expression of our greatest living artists. It <u>needs</u> the opportunity to rub elbows with World musicians and vice versa.

One of the "brilliant boys we sent to India" was Jon Higgins, class of 1962. Higgins literally became a legend in India for giving highly skilled concerts of the local classical music; to this day, stories circulate around his name. It was not easy for Higgins to be far away in South India, as he says in a letter to Winslow; it is from Jon's third year abroad, a long time to be away from Wesleyan, but clearly worth the effort:

Thanks for remembering me, way out here! Had I received the same letter a month ago, I would probably would have completely broken down at your description of late summer New Hampshire afternoons. I went through a bitter siege of homesickness and discouragement. But last week I got the badly needed boost—

*a real affirmation that my steady (well <u>reasonably</u> steady) hard work as a
musician over the past two years has been fruitful, and is bringing me substantial
gains in musicianship—along with some heady professional acclaim.*

At Wesleyan, Higgins was involved in many forms of music; a picture from 1967
shows him with student colleagues, apparently singing early music with lute and
medieval harp.

Jon Higgins
and student
group, 1967.

43

This photo shows Jon Higgins in concert, with T. Ranganathan on the *mrdangam* drum. "Ranga" was the very first artist invited from abroad to teach at Wesleyan in 1962, and the photo below shows him with his brother, T. Viswanathan, the leading light of South Indian (Karnatak) music for decades at Wesleyan until his death in 2000. On top of a Wesleyan Ph.D., "Viswa" received both the President's Award in India and the National Heritage Fellowship of the U.S. National Endowment for the Arts, an unparalleled achievement.

T. Ranganathan, 1960s.

Left to right:
T. Ranganathan,
T. Viswanathan,
P. Srinivasan,
V. Thyagarajan,
early 1970s.

The South Indian tradition is the longest running of any at Wesleyan in the post-1960 era. The faculty in the early twenty-first century consists of David Nelson, a student of T. Ranganathan's, and T. Balusbrahmaniyam, from Chennai, South India, who studied with T. Viswanathan for many years.

The Karnatak Team:
David Nelson and
T. Balusubrahmaniyam,
2008.

Nelson, himself once a Wesleyan undergrad, talks about the continuity of this wing of Wesleyan's World Music Program:

> It was 1962 that the program was first initiated, and the first visiting artist was my teacher, T. Ranganathan, so we've had a continuous presence of South Indian music for more than forty years. It's been strictly this family's lineage, the Dhannamal family. T. Viswanathan, my teacher's brother, was the cornerstone for 25 years, and their sister Balasaraswati would come in the summers sometime.
>
> We [he and Balusubrahmaniyam] feel honored to be carrying on this tradition, and doing it here at Wesleyan. We're sitting in the room that, since this arts complex was constructed, has always been the South Indian room. This is where I worked with my teacher T. Ranganathan, for three years when I was a graduate student, and now, all these years later, I'm the person doing the teaching in this room.

47

It helps the students that they're learning from someone who had to learn it the way they are. There's not so much cultural translation with me. I have done some of that work for them. I think they feel that if I could do it, maybe they can do it too.

Keeping many kinds of music flowing at Wesleyan has always been a logistical, as well as artistic and educational, challenge. The wide varieties of instruments in daily use need repair and replacement. Skins for drumheads from Africa and India are not always readily available, nor are the skills to work on the instruments. In the days when visas for foreign visitors were easier to come by, the music department actually flew in a drum repairman from Madras (now Chennai), which was less expensive than shipping the drums there. Seeing this workman apply his entire body to the process of instrument maintenance—no power tools, please—was a truly educational experience.

Drum repair specialist from Chennai, India, 1991.

The South Indian beginnings of the program coexisted with McAllester's work on Native American traditions. Before 1970 (when women made a comeback as Wesleyan undergrads) the fledgling Anthropology and World Music Programs, along with the Masters of Arts in Teaching Program, allowed female graduate students to take advantage of Wesleyan's offerings. Charlotte Johnson Frisbie recalls:

I enrolled at Wesleyan in the fall of 1962 to work on an M.A. in ethnomusicology. David McAllester and Bob Brown were the major instructors; performance options included the Javanese gamelan and various opportunities in South Indian, once

48

Ranganathan, Ramanathan, Balasaraswati, and the rest of that family arrived. McAllester was teaching several anthropology courses in the Psychology Department, so I added those to the core ethnomusicology courses, tutorials in American Indian studies and Navajo linguistics, work-study jobs in the library and ethnomusicology lab, and an organist job in a nearby town.

Women were new at Wesleyan in 1962, and most of those on campus were in the M.A.T. (Master of Arts in Teaching) Program. The Ethnomusicology program was small; students included Peter Pease, Gerald Johnson, Martin Hatch, and Jon Higgins, as well as myself, and I was the only one focused on American Indian musics. The program required fieldwork, and since McAllester had a grant at the time for a study of Blessingway music, I was given a chance to start working with Navajo singers on one piece of Blessingway hitherto unstudied … the girls' puberty ceremony … that fall, McAllester drove a group of us to the 7th annual meeting [of the Society for Ethnomusicology], my first, at Indiana University in his famous VW bus.

Unidentified
Native
American
musician,
1960s(?).

49

Douglas Mitchell, Navajo Artist in Residence, early 1970s.

David McAllester and Students, 1960s(?).

Frisbie went on to become a distinguished scholar and President of the Society for Ethnomusicology. McAllester continued to enliven the campus with Native American song and dance until 1986. A college guidebook of 1970 cites the Foss Hill powwows as one of the most strikingly distinctive features of Wesleyan's campus life.

By 1965, Winslow was in a strong position to propose adding a Ph.D. in ethnomusicology to the recently chartered M.A. in music. The energy begun with South Indian and Native American music on campus quickly moved into other regions of world music. The Indonesian gamelan ensemble was an inevitable addition, as it was the anchor of the UCLA program that gave Wesleyan Bob Brown. Gamelan was the first imported multicultural style to be integrated into an American

Navaratri Festival: Susan McAllester, Doug Knight, T. Viswanathan, T. Ranganathan, and Namino Torii of Japan, in sari, 1976.

university's musical life. In 1964, Winslow and McAllester drove to the slumping New York World's Fair, held near today's Shea Stadium, to buy the set of instruments that had been brought for the Indonesian Pavilion. Here's the way Winslow tells it:

> *During negotiations, an Indonesian cultural attaché entertained the two Wesleyan professors at lunch in the Indonesian Pavilion where guests were surrounded by native sights, sounds, smells and tastes. Everyone except guests wore native costume. One of the professors noted that the waiter spoke extraordinarily colloquial English, even with an American accent, and he finally said to him, "Excuse me, are you Javanese?" The waiter said, "Are you kidding? I'm from Bahston, the gahden city of America!"*

Wesleyan was lucky to purchase this handsome orchestra at a reasonable rate. Soon, artists from Java joined the department faculty, followed by dancers and graduate students to make Wesleyan a major center of gamelan studies. The adjacent photo was taken at one of the last all-night shadow puppet plays—*wayang kulit*—run by Bob Brown before he left Wesleyan in 1970. Sumarsam arrived in 1972 from Indonesia and has been running the Indonesian music, dance, and theater program ever since.

Bob Brown plays in the gamelan, 1960s.

51

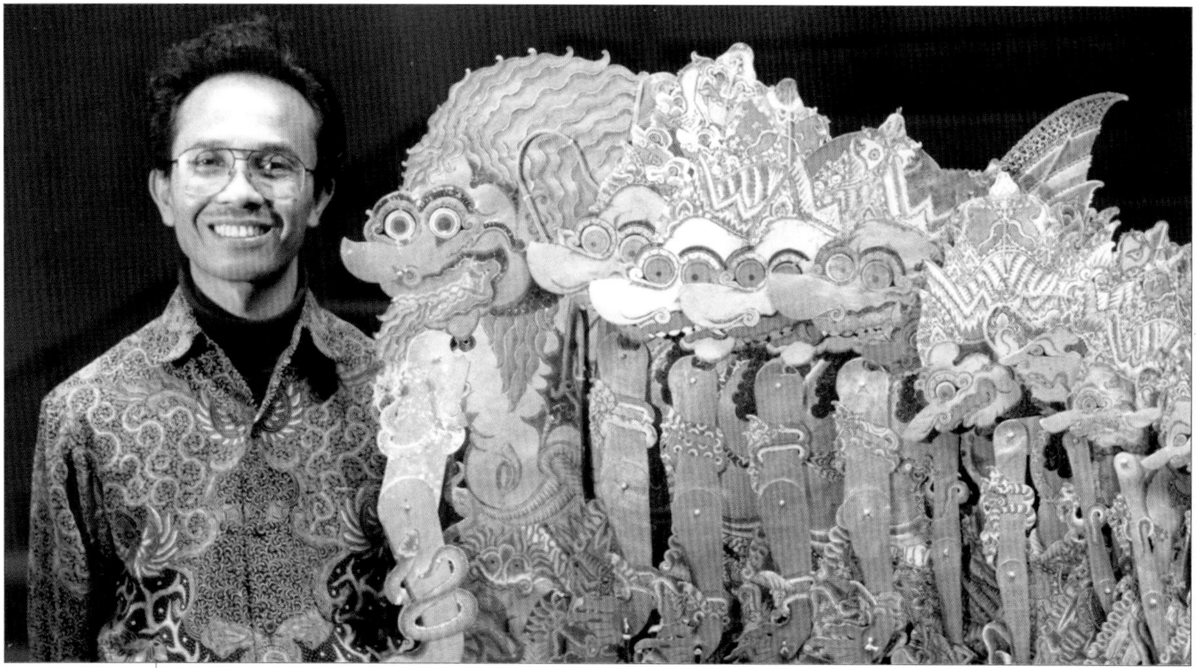

Sumarsam and the *wayang kulit* cast of characters, undated.

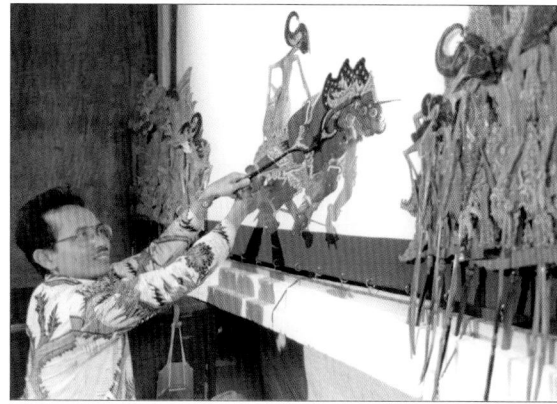

These dramas mostly come from ancient Hindu epics and tell the heroic stories of triumph over demons and evil kings by figures such as Rama who epitomize the virtuous life. Between speeches and action segments, clown figures entertain the audience with ancient and modern humor. A single artist, the *dhalang*, who has to know old and current languages and be able to improvise jokes as well as impart wisdom, runs the whole show. At Wesleyan,

Sumarsam shown at work as the *dalang*, 1991.

the *dhalang* often switches to English to bring the audience into the action. People bring their kids, who might fall asleep and maybe wake up for the noisy action parts, just as they do in Java. Wesleyan *wayangs* are shorter than plays in Java, tending to last only three or four hours instead of stretching until dawn.

The World Music Hall, where the gamelan resides, was the first building on an American campus designed specifically for the performance of global traditions of music and dance, so it has a special place in Wesleyan's national and international profile.

Sumarsam, I. M. Harjito and Karnatak Artist in Residence, Ramnad Raghavan, attend memorial for Ed Blackwell, long-term artist in residence, 1991.

Student gamelan ensemble, 1974. Several students went on to become gamelan and world music specialists. First row *(left to right)*: Gene Leganza, John Minear, Wayne Forrest, Harriotte Hurie, Sam Quigley, Wendy Starr, Laurie Kottmeyer, Alex Dea, Marc Perlman, Tom Alexander, Rick Holmes. Second row *(left to right)*: Nancy Robinson, Anne Mazonson, unknown person, I. M. Harjito (faculty), Allan Robinson, Bill Person, Melissa Blacker, Sumarsam (faculty). Back row *(left to right)*: Michael Kennedy, Bruce Duncan.

Sumarsam came to Wesleyan in 1972 with his wife, Urup Sri Maeny. Sumarsam has been the *dhalang* of Middletown for years, as well as becoming a prominent international scholar with groundbreaking publications; and Maeny teaches Indonesian Dance in the World Dance Program (housed in the Dance Department).

Sumarsam
and Maeny,
undated.

Soon the Music Department's offerings expanded to include African music as one of the "study groups" that combine teaching, research, and performance, a hallmark of the Wesleyan world music experience. The photo below catches a high point in the 1970s, with the presence of Abraham Adzenyah (on the faculty from 1969 until today), his talented colleague, the musician-dancer Freeman Donkor, and Ghanaian graduate student Emanuel Duodu on flute.

Adzenyah has this to say about working with Wesleyan students:

> *Teaching at Wesleyan has been an eye-opener, and it has taught me how to deal with all kinds of people. If you study in Ghana, they give you the instrument and say "play," but they don't tell you how to go inside the music and understand the process.*

> *Some of my students are doing very well. David Locke, senior faculty at Tufts. His students are very enthusiastic. Joe Galeotta teaches at Berklee College of Music in Boston. He goes to Ghana every year with his students. Robert Levin has built a school, from elementary to high school, in Ghana, so he is always going to Ghana.*

Emanuel Duodu, Abraham Adzenyah, Freeman Donkor, 1970s.

African-American music arrived on campus at the same time. Jay Hoggard, a Wesleyan undergrad and now faculty member, gives this history:

> *African-American music was first staffed by Ken McIntyre from 1969 to 1971. From 1971 to 1974, Wesleyan affiliated several outstanding instructors, including Sam Rivers, Jimmy Garrison, Ed Blackwell, and Charles Garner, with trumpeter Clifford Thornton on the faculty during that period. In 1975, Bill Barron arrived as professor. He started the Wesleyan Jazz Orchestra and taught until his death in 1989. Daoud Haroon was artist in residence in the mid-1970s, followed by Dick Griffith and later Bill Lowe, who came around 1980 and stayed until 1990. Anthony Braxton came in 1991. I returned as a graduate student in 1989 and joined the faculty in 1991. I am currently an adjunct associate professor.*

56

Ebony Singers began as a gospel choir under grad student Irene Jackson-Browne in 1973. Undergrads Sam Lowe and Julius Williams continued it in the late 1970s, as did Marichal Monts, who became a department staff member in the 1980s. Fred Simmons, Gary Bennett, Tony Lombardozzi and Roy Wiseman also joined as instructors during the mid-1980s along with Pheeroan Aklaff and Giacomo Gates in the 1990s.

Bill Barron,
Bill Lowe, and
Wesley Brown,
undated.

Jay Hoggard,
undated.

Anthony Braxton conducting one of his operas, 1994.

Anthony Braxton and Ed Blackwell, 1990.

Anthony Braxton brought his unique talent and world stature in 1990, and as of the time of this writing, remains the only Wesleyan faculty member to have received a MacArthur Genius Award.

Graduate
student Royal
Hartigan
shown with
Max Roach,
visiting for the
2000 World
Percussion
Festival, 2000.

Many great African-American musicians taught and played on campus over the years, such as the legendary drummers Ed Blackwell, who also taught private lessons, and Max Roach, who made several appearances.

Meanwhile, more areas of Asian music kept opening up. North Indian (or Hindustani) music was a core part of the program in the early 1970s, before the retrenchment of that era caused cuts in department programs. The adgacent photo catches Sharda Sahai, a renowned *tabla* player with Laxmi Tewari, a graduate student and fine singer.

Japanese music was another victim of the 1970s cuts. It was always a special case in the program because of the way that traditional music teaching works in Japan. The finest performers on

Sharda Sahai on *tabla*, Laxmi Tewari, graduate student vocalist, and unnamed student on *tambura*, 1980s.

the old instruments taught at Wesleyan—*shakuhachi* flute and *koto* zither—run private schools that have the status of music dynasties. To be qualified as a teacher, you have to undergo rigorous training, which westerners know from the martial arts schools. At the pinnacle of the profession, you can be "adopted" into a lineage and take its name, as did many of the musicians who came to Wesleyan. As a result, these artists would tend to stay for a short time only, since they had to tend to their schools back home, a very different set-up than for other world traditions in the department. The photo here is of Namino Torii, still a leading *koto* teacher, with Gen'ichi Tsuge.

Tsuge came as a graduate student and left Wesleyan as a faculty member. His dissertation was not on Japanese music, but the classical styles of Iran, where he did fieldwork. Many of the instruments in Wesleyan's Musical Instrument Collection came to us from Tsuge's travels. He tried to visit every country on the planet. Eventually he went home and became a distinguished professor at Japan's leading arts college.

Namino
Torii, *koto*,
Gen'ichi Tsuge,
graduate
student and
later a faculty
member, with
unnamed
student, 1970s.

From the beginning, Wesleyan combined world music with the related dance forms. The legendary Balasaraswati, sister of the foundational figures T. Viswanathan and T. Ranganathan, came to Wesleyan, as did Lakshmi, Balasaraswati's daughter. Lakshmi carried the tradition into later decades. A photo of 1988 shows her at a recital of *bharata natyam* with her husband and former grad student, Douglas Knight, on drum in the background. Knight has written a book for Wesleyan University Press about Balasaraswati.

Lakshmi dancing, with Douglas Knight, *mrdangam*, and T. Viswanthan, flute, 1980s.

Alongside Javanese and Indian dance, the teaching of African dance is also basic to the Wesleyan curriculum, though it may look different over the decades.

African dance
students,
indoors, 1971.

African dance
students,
outdoors, 2000.

63

As time went on, more and more world music joined the pageant of course offerings and concert life at Wesleyan. Steel Band was one of the highlights of faculty member Gage Averill's time at Wesleyan in the 1990s, and has remained in the program under the aegis of Eric Charry, plus a number of highly talented graduate students.

Gage Averill and the Steel Band, 1996.

Student steel
band, 2008.

Here is Averill's account of the birth of Caribbean music on campus:

February 14, 1992: Carnival bunting, glitter, banners, and fringe cover the spare modernist limestone walls and stage of Wesleyan's Crowell Hall. With a conch shell blast and a call to "lese les bon temps roulez," I begin to throw beads into the audience as a New Orleans–style brass band descends into the auditorium playing a wailing funeral number that quickly morphs into a raucous parade jazz beat. Video cameras trained on the audience members project their own image back to them on monitors arrayed at the side of the stage and in the aisles. Whatever they do—whether they dance or sit passively—their actions will become part of the performance. Above the stage in the organ loft, students from my "Carnival and the Carnivalesque" class are dancing in the costumes they prepared on a theme of "cyborgs and the humanity-devouring potential of technology" (their choice). Their own spectacular participation in dance and masquerade—perched above the stage as though they are enjoying themselves on a carnival reviewing stand—is intended as a model of audience immersion in this multicultural Carnival.

The brass band is followed by a Rio-style samba batucada, two steel bands, a Haitian community dance troupe, a Cuban-style carnival comparsa band (and rumba group), a visiting Brazilian capoeira group, and a Haitian-style rara band; each of these groups has dancers, a chorus, percussionists, singers, and other instrumentalists. They follow each other without a break or intermission, often overlapping in acoustic spheres. Names of my own bands purposely accentuate the sense of something out of control: "Rara Blan Fou Yo" (Rara of the Crazy Foreigners), "Pandemonium Steelband," and "Con-Fusion Brass Band," for example.

I was hired at Wesleyan University in 1990 after a year teaching at Columbia University (which had no performance program). I was told during the hiring process that the current faculty viewed my appointment as a possible bridge to the students and that it was hoped that I would direct an ensemble. This was unique at Wesleyan, where all the other ensembles were directed by "culture bearers" (master artists) rather than by North American academicians.

One day I encountered an old set of steel pans under a stairwell at Wesleyan. They had been donated to the school a decade earlier and had been briefly used by a student-led ensemble in the mid-1980s. By 1990 they had degenerated into a mismatched, out-of-date, and terribly rusted set, and a couple of the barrels were used to store mops by the custodians. I held a pan-refurbishing party and contracted with a local tuner to get them playable and to hold a workshop on pan. I had only minimal pan experience (sitting in with a Seattle band) but I had listened to steel bands since I was five years old, and it dawned on me that such an ensemble could function as a centerpiece in a broad program of Caribbean music studies, forming a link to my own curricular offerings ("Caribbean Music" and "Carnival and the Carnivalesque," among other courses).

The "old set of steel pans" was actually new to Wesleyan at the time. They came as the result of a phone call from Greenwich-based Conoco Oil Corporation, telling the chair of music that the company had disbanded its executives' ensemble and wanted to donate the instruments to a Connecticut college. The department took the somewhat shopworn instruments, which were just waiting under the stairwell for someone like Gage Averill to bring them to life for students. This accidental acquisition is one of many in Wesleyan's World Music Collection, the largest assemblage of any liberal arts college, with over 500 instruments. This grouping includes not just the odd donation,

The Wesleyan musical instrument collection, 2008.

but systematic acquisitions by faculty for demonstration and ensemble use, a remarkable mixture of practical, everyday teaching tools and archival treasures.

The Virtual Instrument Museum (VIM) is a multimedia website (www.wesleyan.edu/music/vim) created by Eric Charry, together with Wesleyan's ITS staff, that introduces a worldwide audience both to the Wesleyan collection and to concepts of organology (the study of musical instruments). Various campuses and museums use the website, which is highly regarded as innovative. Several undergraduate and graduate alumni have gone on to work with musical instruments, notably Sam Quigley at the Boston Museum of Fine Arts, Fred Stubbs, Dennis Waring, and Tom Randall.

THE EXPERIMENTAL MUSIC TRADITION EXPANDS

The Wesleyan music vision of the new era was not just about world music. As his 1966 report to the Trustees shows, Richard Winslow had made it clear that the new experimental music forms pioneered by John Cage and others had to have a significant presence on campus. In 1969, Alvin Lucier first visited, and then joined the faculty, opening up a new dynamic phase of music composition and performance. The urge for a worldwide expression of sound experimentation combined with a homegrown American streak of radicalism was a perfect match for Wesleyan's new approach.

Lucier has developed his own sonic world, working closely with the actual performing spaces in which the music is performed. In his classic piece "I Am Sitting in a Room," the composer's short statement is taped, played back, then taped again in a repeating series that slowly succumbs to the room tone of the space; speech dissolves into pulsed sound as the playback-record cycle takes on the character of the room.

Lucier remembers the early days of experimental music this way:

> When I first came to Wesleyan—part time in the spring semesters of 1968 and 1969, and full time 1970—the space where the CFA is now was a field with a barn in it. We used to hold classes in that barn. There was no electronic equipment there at that time although I did find a Kenwood home audio amplifier in one of the rooms. My first class had about a dozen undergraduates. We made pieces with found objects—coke bottles and such. In that class several of the students went on to careers in music: John Fulleman worked for many years as a sound engineer for the Merce Cunningham Dance Company. He also collaborated with

69

John Cage by recording sounds of Dublin for Roaratorio and collaborated with me on a solar-powered sound installation in the then Farmers & Mechanics Bank in Middletown. Peter Zummo is an active composer and performer living in New York; John Pemberton is currently an ethnomusicologist teaching at Columbia, and Doug Simon is president of Studio Consultants, a flourishing company in New York that supplies recording studios with high-end mixers and amplifiers and loudspeakers.

I remember our first concert in the Chapel. It must have been in 1970. Composer Christian Wolff came down from Dartmouth where he was teaching Classics and Music. The program consisted of Toshi Ichiyanagi's "Distance." As we passed North College we played our instruments from far away. Performers dangled bows and garden hoses down from the balcony to play their instruments positioned on the ground floor. Christian performed his "Electric Spring" during which he crawled down the aisle dragging an electric guitar. We also performed a piece of John Cage's—I don't remember which—and my "Vespers." This was the first of numerous experimental music concerts at Wesleyan. Present-day graduate students still use the Chapel to give concerts of their [experimental and conventional] works.

We used to take classes to Hurd State Park and Dooley Pond in Middletown to record environmental sounds as material for original compositions. Early spring peepers on trails in Wadsworth Park were often fruitful. Once an entire class climbed trees around Dooley Pond armed with tape recorders.

Often the class before Thanksgiving was under-attended—students would leave a day or so early to get home for Thanksgiving. On these occasions I would take *my class on a mystery tour down to the Farmers & Mechanics Bank to check out "Solar Sounder," a sound installation I had mounted in the foyer of the bank. One year as we passed by North College we all traipsed into Bro Adams' office to wish him Happy Thanksgiving [Adams was an assistant to President Chace]. I knew he would be apprehensive to have 50 students drop into his office. Those were the days when students would occupy administration offices as forms of protest. We merely wanted to scare him a little. Adams, somewhat relieved, took it with a sense of humor.*

Lucier was joined by Ron Kuivila, a Wes alum who returned as faculty. Kuivila, a pioneer in computer composition of music, worked up Wesleyan's studio and has encouraged students to push the limits of technology to create experimental music in many formats, including numerous installation events around campus and in town.

Alvin Lucier and Ron Kuivila, electronic music studio, 1980s.

The experimental music tradition has often intersected with world music activity in the composition and performance of many works, such as the gamelan collaboration shown below.

By the mid-1990s, generations of Wesleyan music graduate students had taken positions on many campuses and in countries around the world. A photo from one of the reunions shows David McAllester, Richard Winslow, Betty Winslow, T. Viswanathan, and Abraham Adzenyah with a fine cross-section of former students. A roster of places where undergraduate and graduate alumni hold positions includes Yale, Stanford, Amherst, Brown, Cornell, Duke, Trinity, Wheaton, Tufts, Hampshire, Kenyon, Gettysburg, Rider, New England Conservatory, Lewis & Clark, Rensselaer Polytechnic Institute, the Universities of Massachusetts, Wisconsin, Alabama, California, Oklahoma, North Carolina, New York, and New Haven, as well as abroad in many countries, including China, India, South Korea, Taiwan, Hong Kong, Malaysia, Indonesia, the United Kingdom, Switzerland, Germany, Ghana, Australia, and South Africa.

Graduate alumni gathering (*left to right*): first row, Mirjana Lausevic, Barbara Benary, Jay Pillay, McAllester, Viswanathan, Paul Berliner, and Marc Perlman; second row, Tom Ross and Ed Herbst; third row, Adzenyah, unknown person, Michael Kaloyanides, and unknown; back row, unknown, unknown, Wayne Forrest, and Robert Labaree, 1997.

Mark, Greta, and Maya Slobin shown with graduate students, 1972.

Music diplomacy on the steps of Russell House: Mark Slobin with distinguished American and Soviet ethnomusicologists, 1989.

The campus has also been the scene of many important gatherings of music scholars, such as the 1989 Soviet-American ethnomusicology summit.

Part of the concept of "world music the Wesleyan way" is that all forms are equal, including those of the traditions most students have grown up with. Choirs and choruses of all sort continue to sprout on campus, from the large network of informal a cappella groups through department-sponsored organizations such as Wesleyan Singers, Concert Choir, Ebony Singers (under Marichal Monts), and Collegium Musicum (under Jane Alden).

Neely Bruce and Wesleyan Singers: carols at the President's House, 1998.

Virginia Hancock
and the Concert
Choir, 1985.

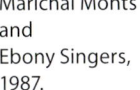

Marichal Monts
and
Ebony Singers,
1987.

Jane Alden
and
Collegium
Musicum,
2005.

Mel Strauss and harpsichordist Igor Kipnis with Wesleyan Orchestra, undated.

Angel Gil-Ordoñez, 1990s.

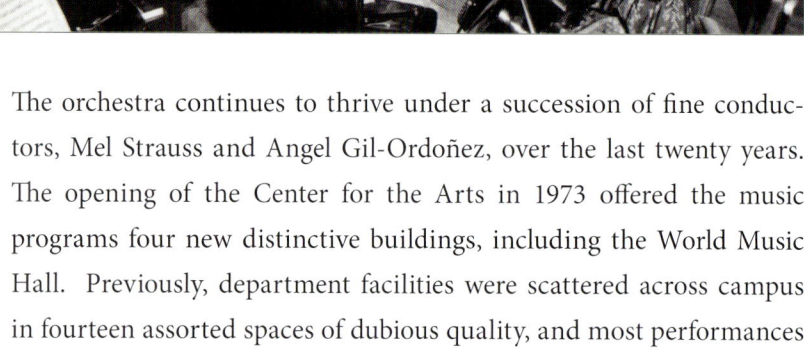

The orchestra continues to thrive under a succession of fine conductors, Mel Strauss and Angel Gil-Ordoñez, over the last twenty years. The opening of the Center for the Arts in 1973 offered the music programs four new distinctive buildings, including the World Music Hall. Previously, department facilities were scattered across campus in fourteen assorted spaces of dubious quality, and most performances could only be held in the Memorial Chapel.

Wesleyan faculty member David Schorr's poster for the Mozart opera performance marking the grand opening of the Center for the Arts, 1973.

a *theatre/music department* production in dedication of the Walter A. **Crowell Concert Hall** / the *Center for the Arts* / Wesleyan University

CosiFanTutte

by Wolfgang Amadeus **Mozart** / libretto by Lorenzo DaPonte / English version by Ruth and Thomas **Martin** / musical director, Raymond E. **Rendall** / conductor, Richard K. **Winslow** / stage director, Ralph D. **Pendleton** October **26**th and **27**th / **8:00** pm / tickets: student **$3**, non-student **$5**, **box office opens** October 15 in the Gallery, Center for t

Thousands of students have enrolled for private lessons through the Music Department, which relies on a large corps of teachers on a huge range of instruments to allow undergrads to continue or start new musical adventures. One such teacher who has been here for decades is flutist Peter Standaart, shown here with other private lessons teachers.

One student of the class of '78, Michael Roth, took jazz piano lessons through Wesleyan's Music Department. When he became the president of Wesleyan University, he chose to conclude his inauguration with a performance of a jazz standard.

Peter Standaart with Libby Van Cleve and Britt Wheeler at the Alsop House, 1980s.

President Michael Roth caps his inauguration ceremony with a turn at the jazz piano, 2007.

No account of music at Wesleyan can leave out the permanent presence of organ. In the early decades, organ was both part of the required chapel attendance experience and an instrument for visiting virtuosos at recitals. In the 1990s, the renovation of the Memorial Chapel allowed for the installation of a new organ, all overseen by University organist Ronald Ebrecht.

Ron Ebrecht
at the
Chapel organ,
undated.

The post-1960 era saw more intense music making that spilled well beyond the borders of the Music Department. In 1961, a group of seniors not only formed a folk singing group on campus, but saw their hit single climb the pop music charts. The Highwaymen—Robert Burnett, Stephen Butts, Chandler Daniels, David Fisher, and Stephen Trott, all class of '62—were honor students and fraternity brothers. By July, *Billboard* magazine voted the Highwaymen "the year's most promising band." Even though they stayed at school rather than go on the road, they split more than $100,000 that year (in 1961 dollars). As Fisher recalls, "It was a lot of fun being in school and being the number-one group. We did concerts three days a week. Every weekend we were gone from Friday morning until Sunday night." They all managed to graduate with honors, with Burnett being vice president of his class and captain of the track team. Trott left the band first, to go to Harvard Law School, and ended up as a federal judge. The band has held sporadic reunion events over the decades. The Highwaymen left their mark on the music of the era, as the All Music Guide explains:

Apart from a couple of major hit singles, and appearances on The Ed Sullivan Show, they contributed a couple of future standards to the folk repertory ("Big Rock Candy Mountain," "All My Trials"), played a key role in the unearthing of a major overlooked Leadbelly song, which later became a major new addition to the repertories of both Creedence Clearwater Revival and the Beach Boys, and also made the first recordings, or the first American recordings, of seminally important songs by Buffy St. Marie and Ewan McColl, respectively.

The Highwaymen, 1961.

Telegram looking for campus photo of The Highwaymen, 1961.

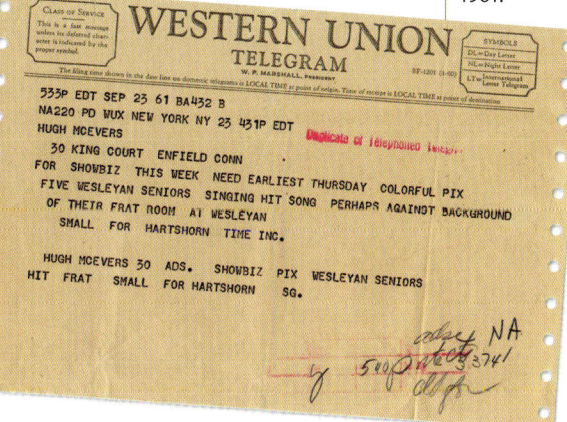

ESDAY, MAY 6, 1970   THE WESLEYAN ARGUS   page five

nday...

Jerry Garcia

Robert A. Rosenbaum, member
of the Kingman Brewster fan club.

Mrs. Colin G. Campbell

Photo Essay by Bud Spurgeon and
A. A. Feinstein
Aerial Photo by Howard Borgstrom

Mike Miller & Friends

Argus 5/6/70

Perhaps the most celebrated musical event of the early post-1960 era was an appearance in May 1970 of the Grateful Dead on Foss Hill, which the *Argus* covered with dramatic photographs and a description with a bit of an academic slant:

Several Wesleyan faculty members [from the Sociology Department, led by Professor Phil Ennis, who later wrote a book on rock-n-roll], assisted by fifteen students, filmed, taped, interviewed and observed the crowd.

Cross Street Market [later the Neon Deli] reported heavy sales of soda, donuts, and other inexpensive consumables. By 3:30 all toys selling for less than thirty-nine cents and all candy had been bought. Much of that, including bags of bubble gum, was indiscriminately lofted to the crowd … Balloons, beach balls and toy soldiers arrived with members of the Hog Farm Commune in the People's Park Bus, and 1000 oranges were donated by West College.

Many deemed themselves "Dead freaks" and came just for the music. Others who had been, or wished they had been, at Woodstock arrived to live or relive the occasion.

Singing around the piano, undated.

Despite enormous social and musical changes of the late 1960s and early 1970s, the informal singing traditions never left the campus. Men in fraternity living rooms kept singing around the piano.

"The New Group," a mixed a cappella group, undated.

Singing groups such as the Jibers gave way to the new a cappella groups, which now included women.

One only wonders what Mr. Hubbard and Mr. Harriman, of the 1862 Glee Club that climbed Mt. Washington, would think of these changes in campus singing groups. Being adventurous and fun loving, perhaps they would first be fazed, but then join in the fun.

Left to right: Mr. Harriman and Mr. Hubbard of the 1862 Glee Club, 1862.

The African *kora*: Eric Charry and graduate student Nicholas Hockin, 2008.

NEWER WORLD MUSIC TRADITIONS

With new waves of faculty and student interest, music at Wesleyan keeps expanding and morphing over time. For example, African music has expanded from West African drumming to include the string *kora* tradition under the guidance of Eric Charry.

Taiko drumming at
commencement,
2008.

Korean Ensemble,
2008.

Most recently, the campus has seen a flowering of East Asian musical traditions. From Japan, long absent from music at Wesleyan, *taiko* drumming pulsates with new energy.

Korean traditional music has also blossomed on campus.

87

Zheng
Xiaoying
conducting
at Wesleyan,
2000.

Wesleyan's ancient ties to China, rooted in the recent Freeman initiatives, have flowered musically through the efforts of faculty member Su Zheng, originally from China, who has a Ph.D. from Wesleyan. Her mother, Zheng Xiaoying is a celebrated orchestra and opera conductor whose likeness even graces a Chinese postage stamp. In 2000, she came to Wesleyan to work with the orchestra, which performed contemporary Chinese symphonic works.

Past and present Chinese graduate students Li Guangming, Wu Wenguang, and Min Yang pictured with Su Zheng and Mark Slobin, Beijing, 2007.

Chinese Ensemble, 2008.

Departmental faculty members have traveled to China as part of an ongoing relationship with the Central Conservatory of Music, the country's premiere arts college.

This kind of renewal keeps music at Wesleyan alive with energy after more than 175 years. In 1966, Richard Winslow predicted, "Within ten years our example will have been widely emulated and within twenty-five years it will have become a norm." Wesleyan has become a model, but even in the twenty-first century, the Wesleyan way has not become the norm. Wesleyan University still stands out for its adventurous and infectious multiplicity and enthusiasm. Music at Wesleyan will always be lively, diverse, and even hectic at times. This small panorama of over one and three-quarter centuries of music at Wesleyan has highlighted only some of its amazing range of trends, groups, and personalities.

Mark Slobin is a professor of music at Wesleyan University. He is the author of *Fiddler on the Move: Exploring the Klezmer World* (2000) and *Subcultural Sounds: Micromusics of the West* (1993, 2000), and editor of *Global Soundtracks: Worlds of Film Music* (2008).

Richard K. Winslow '40 is John Spencer Camp Professor of Music, emeritus, at Wesleyan University. Called a "true original" by colleagues, he is a prolific composer who also had the vision to imagine Wesleyan's World Music Program and the organizational skills to establish it. His compositions—referred to by fellow faculty members as "seductive"— range widely from functional music for the Wesleyan Glee Club (which he conducted) to large-scale operas and oratorios to works for plays by Gertrude Stein and Samuel Beckett. Winslow received a Guggenheim Fellowship in composition in 1956 and Wesleyan's Distinguished Alumnus Award in 1970.